SCOOBY-DOO!

BEGINNER MYSTERIES

STONE ARCH BOOKS
a capstone imprint

Published in 2017 by Stone Arch Books, A Capstone Imprint
1710 Roe Crest Drive, North Mankato, Minnesota 56003
www.mycapstone.com

Library of Congress Cataloging-in-Publication Data
Cataloging-in-publication information is on file with the
Library of Congress.
ISBN: 978-1-4965-4768-2 (library binding)
ISBN: 978-1-4965-4772-9 (paperback)
ISBN: 978-1-4965-4776-7 (eBook PDF)

Editorial Credits:
Editor: Alesha Sullivan
Designer: Brann Garvey
Art Director: Nathan Gassman
Media Researcher: Wanda Winch
Production Specialist: Katy LaVigne
Design Elements:
Warner Brothers design elements, 1, 4-7, 106-112
The illustrations in this book were created by Scott Jeralds

Printed and bound in the United States of America.
010400F17

SCOOBY-DOO!

BEGINNER MYSTERIES

CREEPY COWBOY CAPER

by Michael
Anthony Steele

illustrated by
Scott Jeralds

TABLE OF CONTENTS

P9-DED-407

MEET MYSTERY INC.

SCOOBY-DOO

SKILLS: Loyal; super snout
BIO: This happy-go-lucky hound avoids scary
situations at all costs, but he'll do anything
for a Scooby Snack!

SHAGGY ROGERS

SKILLS: Lucky; healthy appetite
BIO: This laid-back dude would rather look for grub than search for clues, but he usually finds both!

FRED JONES, JR.

SKILLS: Athletic; charming
BIO: The leader and oldest member of the gang. He's a good sport — and good at them, too!

DAPHNE BLAKE

SKILLS: Brains; beauty
BIO: As a sixteen-year-old fashion queen, Daphne solves her mysteries in style.

VELMA DINKLEY

SKILLS: Clever; highly intelligent
BIO: Although she's the youngest member of Mystery Inc., Velma's an old pro at catching crooks.

CHAPTER ONE

FRIGHTFUL WARNING

The Mystery Machine drove down the thin desert road. The setting sun hung low in the sky. The van left a thin cloud of dust as it zipped along.

"Yep, there's no doubt about it," said Fred as he drove. "We're definitely lost."

"I think you're right," agreed Daphne. She looked at a large map. "I can't find where we are at all."

"Like, we have bigger problems," added Shaggy.

"What's that?" asked Velma.

"Scooby and I are late for our predinner snack," replied Shaggy.

Scooby nodded his head. His long tongue flapped from the side of his mouth. "Reah, reah!"

GURGLE! Scooby's stomach rumbled.

GURRRRGLE! Shaggy's stomach rumbled louder.

"My stomach agrees with your stomach, Scoob," said Shaggy.

"Look!" Daphne pointed through the windshield. "There's an old house up there."

Up ahead, a small wooden house sat just off the road. A bearded man sat in a rocking chair on the front porch.

"Good eye, Daphne," said Fred. "We can stop and ask for directions."

The Mystery Machine pulled up beside the old house.

Fred poked his head out the window. "Excuse me, sir. Can you help us? I think we're lost."

The man sprang from his chair. "Jedediah Brooks at your service," said the man. "Happy to help!"

"Can you tell us how to get back to the main highway?" asked Fred.

"Sure thing, kids," said the man. He turned and squinted at the road ahead. "You drive up yonder a ways. Then when you get to the fork in the road, you go right."

GURRRGLE! GURRRRRGLE! Shaggy's stomach growled.

Mr. Brooks looked at the front of the Mystery Machine. "You having car trouble or something?"

Velma laughed. "No, just some hungry passengers."

Daphne looked at the map. "I think I know where we are. If we take a left at the fork, we'll go into Sladeville. Right?"

"Sladeville?" asked Shaggy. "Like, maybe they have a burger joint there or something."

Mr. Brooks' eyes widened. "Oh, you kids don't want to go to Sladeville. That there is just an old ghost town."

"A ghost town?!" asked Shaggy and Scooby-Doo together.

The entire van started to shake as Scooby-Doo and Shaggy shivered in fear.

Mr. Brooks eyed the Mystery Machine again. "Are you sure there's nothing wrong with your van?"

"Oh, that's just Shaggy and Scooby again," explained Velma. "They don't know that a ghost town is just an old, empty town. It's not full of real ghosts."

"Normally I would agree with you," said Mr. Brooks. "But folks in these parts say that the ghost of the *outlaw* Eli Slade roams the streets of Sladeville."

"They named the town after an outlaw?" asked Daphne.

"No, ma'am," replied Mr. Brooks. "The story goes that Eli Slade came into town one day and took over the place. Made them change the name of the town and everything."

The gang looked at Mr. Brooks curiously.

Mr. Brooks squinted at them. "I'd steer clear of Sladeville if I were you."

CHAPTER TWO

GHOST TOWN

Fred drove the Mystery Machine
until they reached the fork in the
road. He hit the brakes. They had a big
decision to make.

"Okay, gang," said Fred. "What'll it be? Do we head for the highway or check out this ghost town?"

"I've always wanted to see a real ghost town!" said Velma.

"Me too," agreed Daphne.

"Like, I vote that we head for the highway," said Shaggy.

"Ree too," agreed Scooby-Doo.

"Oh, come on, you two," said Daphne. "You don't really believe that spooky story, do you?"

Scooby nodded. "Reah, reah!"

Velma pulled out a brightly colored cardboard box. She gave it a shake. "Would you do it for a Scooby Snack?"

Scooby-Doo shook his head. "Uh-uh!"

Velma shook the box again. "Would you do it for *two* Scooby Snacks?"

Scooby thought for a moment and then smacked his lips. "Rokay!"

Velma reached into the box and pulled out two Scooby Snacks. She tossed them into the back of the van.

Scooby-Doo snatched one of the treats out of the air with his mouth. But before he could get the other one, Shaggy leaned forward and gobbled it up.

"Like, learn to share, eh Scoob?" asked Shaggy.

Scooby sighed. "Rokay."

"That settles it," said Fred. He hit the gas and took the road on the left.

It wasn't long before the Mystery Machine passed an old sign. The faded letters read: *Welcome to Sladeville.* As they drove closer they could see several old buildings in the dimming sunlight.

"Wow, it looks like a real Wild West town," said Daphne.

"Except a lot spookier," added Shaggy.

The Mystery Machine slowly drove down the street. It passed a rundown bank, a dentist office, and a general store. The signs were faded and all the windows were broken. It looked as if no one had been there for a long, long time.

"I think Mr. Brooks was wrong," said Velma.

"Good," said Shaggy. "I don't want to run into the ghost of Eli Slade."

"I mean wrong about this being a ghost town," explained Velma. "Look."

She pointed to a large building on the corner. It was the old dance hall. Light shown out of its windows and open doorway. The sound of piano music filled the air.

"It sounds like someone is having a party," said Fred. "Let's check it out."

They pulled to a stop in front of the old building. Fred, Velma, and Daphne climbed out of the van. Scooby-Doo and Shaggy stayed inside.

"Like, I'll stay here and watch the Mystery Machine," said Shaggy.

"Ree too," agreed Scooby-Doo.

"If that's what you want," said Daphne. "But a party usually means snacks."

Suddenly Scooby-Doo and Shaggy appeared outside the van in front of the others. "What are we waiting for?" asked Shaggy.

Shaggy and Scooby-Doo led the way as they walked down the sidewalk. When they reached the entrance, everyone peered inside. The room was full of men in cowboy hats and women in long dresses.

"Look at those *costumes*," said Velma. "They must be having a Wild West party."

The gang stepped inside, and they made their way through the crowd. No one seemed to notice them.

Scooby-Doo spotted a woman carrying a tray full of cheese and crackers. He followed her and reached out to grab a tasty snack. Surprisingly, his paw passed right through the tray. Scooby tried again and the same thing happened. It was as if the woman was a …

Scooby gulped. "A rhost!" He ran back to the others. "Raggy! Raggy!"

"What is it, Scoob?" Shaggy asked.

Scooby-Doo was so scared that he couldn't speak. He pointed back at the woman. "She's a … She's a …"

"Come on, Scooby," said Daphne. "The snack couldn't have been that bad."

"Let's see if anyone minds us crashing the party," said Fred. He walked up to the nearest cowboy.

"Excuse me, sir." Fred reached out to tap the cowboy on the shoulder. His hand passed right through him.

"Whoa!" Fred stumbled back in alarm. He almost bumped into another cowboy. Instead of bumping into him, Fred passed through him.

Just then everyone in the dance hall turned to look at the Mystery Inc. gang. The ghosts stared at them with glowing red eyes.

Nok-nok-nok-nok! Shaggy's knees knocked together. "Like, they're all ghosts!"

"Let's get out of here!" shouted Daphne.

CHAPTER THREE

CREEPY CHARACTERS

Scooby and Shaggy ran down the dark street. They ducked into an alley and hid behind a stack of wooden crates.

"Like, where did everyone go?" asked Shaggy.

Scooby-Doo looked around and shrugged. "I don't row."

Shaggy and Scooby-Doo tiptoed down the alley back the way they had come. They both peeked their heads around the corner. The street was empty and quiet.

"Maybe they're back at the Mystery Machine," Shaggy suggested.

Scooby-Doo's teeth chattered. "What about the rhosts?"

"It looks like the coast is clear," Shaggy said. "Let's go."

They stepped out of the alley and tiptoed down the sidewalk. They stopped to hide behind every post, barrel, and crate as they walked.

Shaggy pointed to the nearby van. "Let's make a break for it, buddy."

Just as they stepped out from behind their hiding place, a dark figure appeared between them and the van. Shaggy and Scooby stopped in their tracks.

"Fred? Is that you?" asked Shaggy.

The figure stepped forward and into the moonlight. It was a man wearing a black cowboy hat, a tattered black vest, and black cowboy boots. He had a long, black beard and glowing green skin.

"What are you doing in my town?" asked the man.

"*Your* town?" asked Shaggy. "That must mean you're..."

"Rely Rade!" finished Scooby.

"The ghost of Eli Slade," said Shaggy.

"That's right," said the ghost. "And no one comes to Sladeville and lives to tell the tale."

"Let's get out of here, Scooby!" yelled Shaggy.

Shaggy and Scooby-Doo raced down the street and headed for an open doorway. They ducked under a tooth-shaped sign and went inside.

Shaggy and Scooby dove for the chair in the center of the room. They covered themselves with a large white cloth and shivered as they hid. Boots clumped on the sidewalk outside. The ghost of Eli Slade ran past.

"Be with you boys in a minute," said a voice in the room. Scooby and Shaggy peeked out from under the cloth. They saw a man with his back to them.

"Like, this town isn't deserted after all, Scoob," said Shaggy.

"Reah," agreed Scooby.

The man turned to face them. He wore a tattered white coat and held a large pair of pliers.

The ghost had glowing green skin and a wide grin spread across his face. He stared at them with glowing red eyes.

"Zoinks!" yelped Shaggy. "A ghost dentist!"

The ghost dentist loomed closer. "We'll have all those pesky teeth out in no time."

The dentist chair rattled as Shaggy and Scooby shivered in fear.

"Like, I need all my teeth to eat," said Shaggy.

"Ree too!" agreed Scooby.

Scooby-Doo ducked under the sheet as the ghost dentist moved closer.

The ghost jabbed the snapping pliers forward. Shaggy ducked, and the pliers missed with a loud snap. Scooby's head popped up. The dentist went for him. Scooby-Doo ducked just in time as the snapping pliers missed his teeth too. Then Shaggy's head popped up again. He ducked just in time once more.

"We can't keep this up forever, Scoob," said Shaggy.

Shaggy and Scooby-Doo sprang from the chair. They ran in midair spinning the chair around in circles. The ghost dentist became tangled with the cloth and landed in the spinning chair.

Shaggy and Scooby ran out the door
and didn't look back.

CHAPTER FOUR

CHILLING CHASE

"Shaggy? Scooby-Doo?" Velma asked. "Daphne? Fred? Where are you guys?"

Velma crept down the dark sidewalk. She got separated from the others and now couldn't find them anywhere.

"I can't believe this ghost town has real ghosts," said Velma. "Ghosts aren't real. There must be a way to explain…"

Suddenly, a figure stepped out of the shadows. He was a bearded man in black tattered cowboy clothes. "You shouldn't have come to my town," he said. "Eli Slade will make sure you don't bother anyone else ever again."

"Eli Slade?" asked Velma. She began to tremble. "But you're… you're…"

"Your doom!" roared the ghostly outlaw.

Velma ducked as the ghost grabbed for her.

She ran down the street and darted
into a rundown barn. The ghost was
close behind. Velma climbed up an old
ladder and hurried into the hayloft.

The outlaw clawed after her. She
leaped through a broken window and
flew toward the ground below. Luckily,
she landed in a soft hay wagon.

Velma adjusted her glasses and grabbed a handful of hay. "What is fresh hay doing in a ghost town? I mean, I'm glad it was here, but … I think this may be a clue."

"Come back here!" shouted the ghost from the window above.

Velma scooted out of the hay wagon and started running. She took off down the street and ducked into a nearby *blacksmith* stand. She peeked out to see if the ghost was still chasing her. It looked as if she lost him. She caught her breath as her heart pounded.

PANK! PANK! PANK! PANK!

"That's not my heart pounding so loudly," whispered Velma. She turned to see a large man beating something with a large hammer. "There's a real blacksmith here?"

The large man spun around. He had green glowing skin and wore a torn black apron. He raised his hammer and charged at her.

"Jinkies! A ghost blacksmith!" screamed Velma.

She ducked out of the way just as the blacksmith attacked. He swung his hammer at her again and barely missed. Velma tried to make a break for the street, but the giant ghost blocked her path.

"I have to find the others and warn them," said Velma.

Velma ducked under the swinging tool once more. She grabbed a pair of long tongs from a workbench and blocked the next blow.
CLANK!

Velma's entire body trembled from the striking hammer. She put the tongs into the burning furnace and pulled out a red-hot horseshoe. She flung it toward the ghostly blacksmith. The spooky smith dropped the hammer and caught the horseshoe.

"Yeee-ow!" yelled the blacksmith. He tossed the burning hot metal from hand to hand. He ran past Velma and dunked his hands and the horseshoe into a large bucket of water.

SSSSSSSSSSSS!

A cloud of steam filled the area. That was just the break she needed. Velma dashed past the blacksmith and escaped into the street.

CHAPTER FIVE

Fred and Daphne froze as they heard the blacksmith's scream from the other side of the ghost town. They ducked behind a large watering *trough*.

"Did you hear that creepy scream?" whispered Daphne.

"I sure did," replied Fred. "I hope it wasn't Shaggy or Scooby. Let's check it out."

The two rose from their hiding spot and jogged down the street. The town was quiet around them. Dead quiet. They stopped to listen again.

"I don't hear anything now," said Fred. "I wonder where that scream came from."

"Wait a minute." Daphne cocked her head. "I hear something else."

Fred listened. "I hear it, too."

A low rumble filled the air. It grew louder with each passing second. *RUMMMMBLE!*

"Is there a big truck coming this way?" asked Fred.

Daphne turned, and her eyes widened. "Jeepers! It's not a truck. Look!"

Fred saw where Daphne was pointing. At the end of the street, a large herd of cattle ran toward them. The cows were black with long, sharp horns. They rushed forward with glowing red eyes.

"Ghost cattle!" screamed Fred and Daphne.

The two ran as fast as they could down the street. The herd gained on them and snorted in anger. The cattle aimed their sharp horns toward Fred and Daphne.

"We can't outrun them," said Fred. "We have to get out of the way!"

The herd was spread across the entire street and onto the sidewalks. There was no place to duck out of the way.

Daphne pointed to a large hotel up ahead. A wooden *balcony* was attached to the building's second floor. "There!"

"Good idea," said Fred. He ran ahead of her and knelt under the deck. He lowered his hands and laced his fingers together. "Remember your gymnastic training?"

"Sure do," replied Daphne.

She leaped forward and landed a foot on Fred's open palms. He lifted her up as she pushed off.

Daphne soared upward, flipped in the air, and landed on the deck above.

Daphne ran to the railing and reached down for Fred. "Your turn," she said. "And you better hurry!" The runaway cattle were almost on top of him.

RUMMMMMMMMMBLE!

Fred jumped up and reached for Daphne's hand. But he didn't get high enough. His hand barely brushed against Daphne's fingertips. Fred tumbled back to the street below.

"Fred!" shouted Daphne. She shut her eyes tight. She couldn't watch her friend get squashed by the runaway herd.

"Whoa!" said Fred's voice from below.

Daphne opened her eyes to see the black cattle running *through* Fred. It was just like the people in the dance hall.

Daphne sighed with relief. Fred was safe. But the rumble seemed to be louder up on the deck. Daphne glanced down and saw a black box attached to the side of the building. The sound of the thundering hooves came from a large speaker inside the box. As the cattle left the town, the rumble slowly faded.

Daphne leaned over the railing. "I think I found a clue," she said.

Fred's eyes widened as he looked just past her. "Me too. Look!" He pointed over her shoulder.

Daphne turned to see a ghostly outlaw standing on the deck next to her.

"Get out of my town!" growled the outlaw.

"Eli Slade?" Daphne asked.

The ghost didn't answer. Instead, he grabbed for her. Daphne ducked under his arms and jumped to the ground below.

"We have to find the others!" shouted Daphne.

Fred and Daphne took off running down the dark street.

CHAPTER SIX

ON THE WRONG TRACK

"Like, a creepy ghost outlaw doesn't have to tell us twice," said Shaggy. "He wants us to get out of town, so we're getting out of town."

"Rabsorutly!" agreed Scooby-Doo.

The two shuffled into the desert just outside of town. The moonlight lit the tall cactus plants around them. A coyote howled in the distance.

Shaggy glanced around and gulped. "Okay, so maybe it's a little spooky out here too."

Nok-nok-nok-nok-nok!

Scooby's knees knocked together. "Reah!"

They traveled farther into the darkness. Shaggy reached back and grabbed Scooby's paw. "Just hold my hand, buddy, so we can stay together." He continued to shuffle forward.

Scooby trembled. "R-R-Raggy?"

"Yeah, Scoob?" asked Shaggy.

"I'm not rolding your rand," replied Scooby-Doo.

Shaggy froze. He let go of what he was holding and felt for his friend. His hand landed on something that was definitely *not* Scooby-Doo.

Shaggy whimpered. "You didn't grow a long beard did you, Scoob?"

Scooby whined. "Uh-uh! Uh-uh!"

Shaggy spun around and touched noses with the ghost of Eli Slade. The outlaw growled.

"Zoinks!" shouted Shaggy. "Like, we're out of town, like you said!"

"Not far enough!" yelled the outlaw. Slade reached forward.

Shaggy shut his eyes tight. "I can't look."

Suddenly, Shaggy felt himself moving. He opened his eyes to see the outlaw getting smaller and smaller. He was moving away from the angry ghost.

Shaggy looked down to see that he was sitting on Scooby-Doo's back. His friend was taking them away from the ghost of Eli Slade.

"Way to come through, pal," said Shaggy. "But where are we going?"

"A race to hide," replied Scooby.

"Where are we going to hide in the desert?" asked Shaggy. Then he looked to where Scooby was headed. They were moving toward an old *mineshaft*.

"Like, I'll take a spooky mine over a ghost any day," gulped Shaggy.

When Shaggy and Scooby reached the mine, they dove into an old mine cart. They ducked down and hid as the ghost outlaw searched the mine entrance.

Shaggy and Scooby heard buckets being thrown around and lanterns being broken. The ghost wasn't giving up. Suddenly, they began to move again. Shaggy and Scooby-Doo peeked out of the cart.

They were rolling down the track into the dark mine!

"Zoinks!" shouted Shaggy. "What did you do, Scoob? We're rolling into the mine!"

Scooby shrugged his shoulders. "I ridn't do ranything."

Scooby and Shaggy hugged each other and screamed. The cart was out of control as it zipped through the long tunnels. Lanterns along the cave walls lit every sharp turn and shaky bridge.

"Like, does this thing have any brakes?" asked Shaggy.

Scooby found a long *lever* at the front of the cart. Scooby-Doo pulled it, and sparks flew from the wheels below. The cart began to slow. "I found the rakes!" shouted Scooby-Doo.

"Forget the brakes, Scoob. Look!" Shaggy pointed to the track behind them.

Another mine cart was speeding toward them. But it wasn't empty. In the cart rode the ghost of Eli Slade!

Scooby released the brake, but it was too late. The ghost's cart slammed into them. The outlaw reached forward and tried to grab Shaggy and Scooby. They ducked under his big hands.

"Like, can't this thing go any faster?" asked Shaggy.

Scooby shook his head. "Uh-uh!"

Shaggy whimpered. "Either the ghost gets us or we crash." He reached out and shook Scooby's paw. "It's been nice knowing you, pal."

"Rou too, Raggy," replied Scooby-Doo. "Rou too."

They hugged each other as the ghost reached for them one more time. But the outlaw leaned on the lever on his own cart. Sparks flew as he hit the brakes. The ghost cart slowed, and Shaggy and Scooby kept going.

"We're saved, Scoob!" yelled Shaggy.

Scooby looked at the track ahead of them. His ears drooped. "Ruh-Roh!"

"*AAAAAAAAH!*"

The friends screamed as the track spun them in three loops, two big drops, and a long corkscrew. Shaggy and Scooby were still screaming and holding each other tight when the cart finally came to a stop. They opened their eyes and saw that they were back outside the mine.

"Come on, Scoob," said Shaggy. "Let's get out of here!"

"Rokay!" agreed Scooby-Doo.

Dizzy from the wild ride, Shaggy and Scooby-Doo zigzagged back toward town.

CHAPTER SEVEN

CREEPY KIDNAPPING

Fred led the way as he and Daphne tiptoed down the sidewalk. The old boards squeaked under each step. They snuck past the general store toward the street corner.

"We haven't seen the ghost of Eli Slade in a while," whispered Fred. "I'll peek around the corner to see if the coast is clear."

"Okay," Daphne whispered back.

As Fred crept toward the corner, the door to the general store opened. Two hands reached out and pulled Daphne inside. The door silently closed.

"I don't see anyone," reported Fred. "Let's keep looking for the others." When there was no reply, he turned back. "Daphne?" She was gone.

Fred walked back the way he'd come. The street and the sidewalk were empty.

A chill ran up Fred's spine. He was all alone in the creepy ghost town.

As Fred looked toward the other side of the street, the door to the general store opened again. Four hands reached for him. Fred's eyes widened as one hand covered his mouth and the others pulled him inside. The door silently shut once more.

Once inside, Fred saw Eli Slade staring down at him.

"Ah! The ghost of Eli Slade!" he tried to shout. But the hand was still covering his mouth.

"It's okay, Fred," said Velma. "That's just a painting."

Daphne removed her hand from his mouth. "Yeah, see?" She shined a flashlight up at Slade's face. Sure enough, it was a large painting of the outlaw. It hung over the main counter of the general store.

Fred sighed in relief. "I'm glad you found us, Velma," he said. "Have you seen Shaggy and Scooby?"

Velma shook her head. "The only things I've seen were a couple of angry ghosts."

"Did you say *ghosts*?" asked Daphne. "As in more than one?"

Velma told them about her run-in with Eli Slade and the ghost blacksmith. Fred and Daphne told her about the runaway ghost cattle.

"That all sounds very spooky," said Velma. I don't think this ghost town is as empty as it looks," she explained. "I found a wagon full of fresh hay. And that blacksmith ghost didn't like holding a red-hot horseshoe."

"And I came across a modern speaker up on the hotel deck," added Daphne.

"There's more to this place than meets the eye," said Velma.

"I think you're right," agreed Fred. "Daphne, shine your flashlight around this place."

The flashlight lit the inside of the general store. For the most part, it looked like a Wild West general store. There were clothes, tools, and dry goods. But there were modern items for sale too.

"Are those T-shirts?" asked Fred. "And ball caps?"

"They sure are," confirmed Velma. She held up a shirt and read the words printed there: *Historic Haunted Sladeville.*

"This is more like a gift shop than a general store," said Daphne.

"I think I know what's going on," said Fred. "Let's find Shaggy and Scooby and get to the bottom of this."

Fred led the way as they left the store. But none of them noticed that the eyes in the painting followed them all the way out.

CHAPTER EIGHT

At the edge of town, two wooden barrels wobbled down the street. Four paws poked out of the bottom of the first barrel. Hands and feet poked out of the second barrel.

"I gotta hand it to you, Scoob," said Shaggy from under the second barrel. "You picked a great hiding place."

"Reah, reah!" agreed Scooby-Doo from under the first barrel. He peeked out through a hole to lead the way.

"We'll sneak our way back to the Mystery Machine," said Shaggy. "And that ghost will be none the wiser."

The two barrels crept right past the ghost of Eli Slade. The outlaw lifted the second barrel.

Shaggy kept crawling along for a moment. Then he stopped and looked up at the outlaw. "Oh, boy," said Shaggy. "This is embarrassing."

The ghost set the barrel down and shot a dark look at Shaggy. The bearded man cracked his knuckles.

Shaggy raised a finger. "Hold that thought." Shaggy zipped away and returned with a third barrel. He now wore a straw hat, a striped shirt, and a thin mustache.

"Step right up! Step right up!" Shaggy pointed to the three barrels on the ground. "Choose the correct barrel and win a prize!"

The outlaw looked confused.

Shaggy pointed a thin cane at the ghost. "You, sir! Care to try your luck?"

Slade looked around and then pointed to himself. "Who? Me?"

"Yes, sir! Of course you, sir!" replied Shaggy. "All you have to do is find the dog and win a prize!"

Shaggy lifted one of the barrels to show Scooby-Doo. The dog gave a cheerful wave. Shaggy lowered the barrel. He began moving the barrels back and forth to try and confuse the outlaw.

"Round and round he goes, where he stops only Scooby-Doo knows!" shouted Shaggy.

Shaggy stopped shuffling the barrels. "Okay, sir. Try your luck!"

The outlaw nervously looked from one barrel to the other. Finally, he chose the barrel on the right. He picked it up, but Scooby wasn't there.

"Oh, bad luck, sir," said Shaggy. "Try again!"

This time, the outlaw lifted the barrel on the left. Scooby wasn't under there either.

"That leaves just one more," said Shaggy.

The ghost excitedly lifted the middle barrel off the ground. He held it high over his head. The outlaw's eyes widened when the dog wasn't under that one either.

"Hee-hee-hee-hee-hee-hee," giggled Scooby. The dog was holding onto the inside of the barrel.

Slade glanced up and growled at Scooby-Doo.

"Like, you found the dog," stated Shaggy. "Now, here's your prize!"

Scooby-Doo slid out of the barrel and past Slade. Then he and Shaggy each grabbed the barrel and slammed it down.

BONK!

The barrel covered the outlaw, pinning his arms to his side.

Shaggy got rid of the costume as he and Scooby ran away. They had to find a better hiding place before the outlaw escaped from the barrel. They dashed into the nearby bank. They leaped over the counter and skidded into the back.

They waited quietly to see if the ghost would follow them. Then a delicious smell filled their noses.

"Like, do you smell what I smell, Scoob?" asked Shaggy.

Scooby-Doo licked his lips. "Reah, reah! Reah, reah!"

Shaggy grinned. "I think we found the perfect hiding place!"

CHAPTER NINE

"Shaggy," whispered Velma. "Scooby-Doo? Where are you?"

Velma, Fred, and Daphne tiptoed down the sidewalk. They had been searching everywhere for the rest of the Mystery Inc. gang.

"You don't think the ghost of Eli Slade got them, do you?" asked Fred.

"I don't think so," said Velma. "And if I'm right, there is no ghost of Eli Slade."

"There isn't?" asked Daphne. "Why's that?"

"Because ..." Velma started to answer. She was stopped by a ghostly *groan*. *Ohhhhhhh!*

Fred shivered. "Oh, boy."

Another groan filled the air. *Oooohhhh!*

"If there's no ghost, then what's that?" asked Daphne.

"Let's find out," said Velma.

They followed the sound of the creepy groans. The sounds led them to an old bank building. When they opened the door, the noise grew louder. *Ooooohhhhh! Ohhhhhh!*

"Are we sure about this?" asked Daphne.

"I'm sure," replied Velma. "Your flashlight, please."

Daphne handed Velma the flashlight as they headed to the back of the building. They stepped behind the counter...

"Shaggy and Scooby?!!" they said all at once.

The two lay on the floor with empty candy wrappers, popcorn buckets, and cotton candy bags. They rubbed their full stomachs as they groaned.

Shaggy looked up. "Oh hey, gang." He let out a small burp. "You can stop looking for a place to eat now."

Scooby rubbed his belly and giggled. "Rots and rots of ropcorn."

"Where did you get all this food?" asked Daphne.

"Like, it was right here in the bank," replied Shaggy. "I guess for safekeeping."

"It didn't keep it very safe," said Fred.

"All this modern food in a Wild West town?" asked Velma. "It's the final clue to the mystery." She turned and headed for the door. "Let's solve this case. And I know just where to start."

Fred and Daphne followed Velma out of the bank. Shaggy and Scooby-Doo slowly followed.

Velma marched down the street to the blacksmith stand. The smith's hammering grew louder as they approached.

Clank! Clank! Clank!

As they neared, the ghostly blacksmith turned and growled at them. He raised his hammer high above his head.

"Zoinks!" said Shaggy. He leaped into Scooby-Doo's arms. "A creepy blacksmith ghost!"

"You're no ghost, are you?" asked Velma.

The green-skinned blacksmith took a step forward and stared at the gang.

Then the blacksmith lowered his
hammer and smiled.

"You're absolutely right!" The man
set down his tool and reached into his
pocket. He pulled out a walky-talky and
brought it to his mouth.

"Show's over," the blacksmith said.
"Company meeting at the blacksmith's."

The Mystery Inc. gang looked around. People exited buildings all over town. Some were dressed in ghostly western costumes, but many wore regular clothes.

Soon the people of Sladeville surrounded the gang.

"So, what did you think?" asked the blacksmith.

"Oh, Hank," said a ghostly woman in a long dress. "They didn't even make it to my haunted dress shop."

She pulled out a cloth and wiped her glowing green face. The glow-in-the-dark makeup came off.

A man dressed as a ghostly miner stepped up. He pointed at Shaggy and Scooby. "I know that these two got to go on the mineshaft roller coaster."

Shaggy clutched his stomach.

"Let's just say, I'm glad I ate *after* that crazy ride."

"So, this is all an amusement park?" asked Daphne.

"What about the ghost cattle?" asked Fred. "And the people in the dance hall?"

"Those would be *holograms*," replied Hank the blacksmith. "They look real, but they're more like 3D movies than anything else."

Hank grinned at the gang.

"So, do you have any suggestions for us?"

"Why would we have suggestions?" asked Velma.

Hank frowned. "Aren't you the amusement park experts we were expecting?"

"Uh, no we're not," replied Fred. "We were just passing through town."

The Sladeville workers groaned with disappointment.

Daphne looked at all the sad faces.

"But ... this is the spookiest place we've visited in a long time," she said.

"And we've been to creepy places all over the world," added Velma. "We're Mystery Inc." She nodded. "It's what we do."

This put everyone back in a good mood.

"That's very kind of you to say," said Hank. "We don't even have all of our actors yet. We're hoping to get someone to play the ghost of the man himself, Eli Slade."

"But we saw him," said Daphne. "He was one of the scariest parts of this whole place."

Hank shook his head. "He wasn't one of our people."

Scooby-Doo gulped. "Rat means ..."

Shaggy shivered. "The ghost of Eli Slade is real!"

CHAPTER TEN

Velma shook her head. "I can't believe the ghost of Eli Slade is real."

"It looks as if we have one more mystery to solve," said Daphne.

"And I have just the idea for a trap," added Fred.

"Like, count me out, Fred," said Shaggy. "I'm tired of being the *bait* for all your traps."

Fred laughed. "Don't worry, Shaggy. This one is very simple." He rested a hand on Scooby's shoulder. "I'll just need Scooby for this trap. It's time for a Wild West showdown!"

Scooby-Doo gulped.

Fred grinned. "All we have to do is go by the bank and the general store."

A few minutes later, the trap was set. Scooby-Doo stepped out into the empty street. He wore a cowboy hat and a large western *poncho*. He slowly walked down the middle of the street. The *spurs* strapped to his back feet clinked with every step.
CLINK. CLINK. CLINK.

Scooby-Doo looked like a real-life cowboy — or cowdog — as he marched along. The rest of the gang and the workers watched from the windows of the shops. Scooby-Doo felt like a real western hero.

Then a dark figure stepped into the street ahead of him. It was Eli Slade. The creepy outlaw slowly walked forward. The two moved closer and closer to each other.

Scooby-Doo stopped in his tracks. Slade did the same. The outlaw frowned. Scooby-Doo's eyes squinted. They stared at each other. Tumbleweeds blew across the street between them.

Scooby threw back his poncho to show he was wearing a cowboy gun belt around his waist. Slade's eyes widened. Then Scooby reached down and drew ... his bananas!

Scooby giggled as the outlaw charged toward him. "Rooby-rooby-doo!"

As Scooby ran away from the ghost, he squeezed the bananas. Each fruit popped out of its skin. Scooby caught them in his mouth and gulped them down. Then he tossed the peels over his shoulder.

Scooby-Doo skidded to a stop as the outlaw closed in. Then Slade stepped on the banana peels and slid out of control. The dog easily stepped to the side as the outlaw zipped past. Slade's arms flew around as he headed straight toward a water trough.

SPLASH!

Suddenly everyone ran out of the buildings. They gathered around the struggling ghost in the trough. Except he wasn't a ghost at all.

The water washed away the glow-in-the-dark makeup and black hair dye. The ghost of Eli Slade was none other than ...

"Jedediah Brooks!" said Fred.

Hank and Shaggy helped the man out of the water. The man sputtered as he got to his feet.

"What are you doing here?" asked Velma.

Mr. Brooks shook his head and said, "Oh, I followed your van to the fork in the road."

Mr. Brooks shrugged.

"When I saw that you went to Sladeville anyway, I snuck into town after you. It wasn't hard to find a costume and makeup so I could become the ghost of Eli Slade."

"But why?" asked Daphne.

Mr. Brooks hung his head.

"I didn't want my little road getting busy after this here amusement park opens. I like sitting on my porch, enjoying the peace and quiet. I thought that if everyone thought there really was a ghost of Eli Slade … well, maybe the park wouldn't open."

Hank placed a hand on Mr. Brooks' shoulder.

"Well, if you'd like to do something besides sitting on your porch all day, maybe you can work for us," said Hank.

The rest of the Sladeville workers nodded in agreement.

"You could play Eli Slade full-time."

Mr. Brooks scratched his head.

"Well, it was fun scaring all these young folks."

He looked up at Hank.

"Does that include free rides on the roller coaster?" He grinned. "That was fun too."

Hank shook Mr. Brooks' hand. "It's a deal!"

Velma's eyes lit up. "Ooh! Can we ride the roller coaster?"

"You bet," said Hank. "Rides all around!"

He led the way as everyone moved toward the edge of town.

"Careful, Velma," warned Shaggy. "It's pretty scary."

"Reah!" agreed Scooby-Doo.

"Don't worry, guys," smiled Velma. "Nothing is too scary for Mystery Inc."

THE END

ABOUT THE AUTHOR

MICHAEL ANTHONY STEELE has been in the entertainment industry for more than 24 years writing for television, movies, and video games. He has authored more than one hundred books for exciting characters and brands, including Batman, Green Lantern, Shrek, LEGO City, Spider-Man, Tony Hawk, Word Girl, Garfield, Night at the Museum, and The Penguins of Madagascar. Mr. Steele lives on a ranch in Texas but he enjoys meeting his readers when he visits schools and libraries all over the country. He can be contacted through his website, MichaelAnthonySteele.com

ABOUT THE ILLUSTRATOR

SCOTT JERALDS has created many a smash hit, working in animation for companies including Marvel Studios, Hanna-Barbera Studios, M.G.M. Animation, Warner Bros., and Porchlight Entertainment. Scott has worked on TV series such as *The Flintstones, Yogi Bear, Scooby-Doo, The Jetsons, Krypto the Superdog, Tom and Jerry, The Pink Panther, Superman,* and *Secret Saturdays,* and he directed the cartoon series *Freakazoid,* for which he earned an Emmy Award. In addition, Scott has designed cartoon-related merchandise, licensing art, and artwork for several comic and children's book publications.

GLOSSARY

BAIT (BAYT)—food used as a trap for catching animals

BALCONY (BAL-kuh-nee)—a platform with railings on the outside of a building or structure; usually on an upper level

BLACKSMITH (BLAK-smith)—a person who makes and fixes things made of iron

COSTUME (KOSS-toom)—clothes someone wears to hide who he os she is

GROAN (GROHN)—to make a long, low sound showing that you are in pain or are unhappy

HOLOGRAM (HOL-uh-gram)—an image made by laser beams that looks three-dimensional (3D)

LEVER (LEV-ur)—a bar or a handle that you use to work or control a machine

MINESHAFT (MINE-shaft)—a deep, narrow hole that gives access to a mine; a mine is a place where workers dig up minerals that are underground

OUTLAW (OUT-law)—a criminal, especially one who is running away from the law

PONCHO (PON-choh)—a cloak that looks like a blanket with a hole in the center for the head; ponchos were originally worn in South America

SPUR (SPUR)—a spike or spiked wheel on the heel of a rider's boot; spurs are used to make a horse go faster or obey commands

TROUGH (TRAWF)—a long, narrow container from which animals can drink or eat

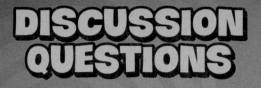
DISCUSSION QUESTIONS

1. What were some of the scariest things Scooby-Doo and the gang discovered in the ghost town of Sladeville? Can you think of some other spooky things they might find?

2. Life sure was different back in the Wild West. What are some things that people did differently back then? What are some of the things that you have now that people didn't have back then?

3. Have you ever been to an amusement park? What was your favorite part of your visit?

WRITING PROMPTS

1. Would you like to have lived in the Wild West?
   Write about some of the things you would do there.

2. Shaggy and Scooby are scared of all kinds
   of things. What are some things that frighten
   you? Write about how you could be brave about
   something that scares you.

3. Sometimes outlaws were bullies in the Wild West.
   Write about why it's bad to be a bully.

LOOK FOR MORE

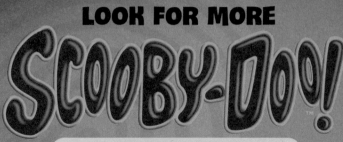

SCOOBY-DOO!

BEGINNER MYSTERIES

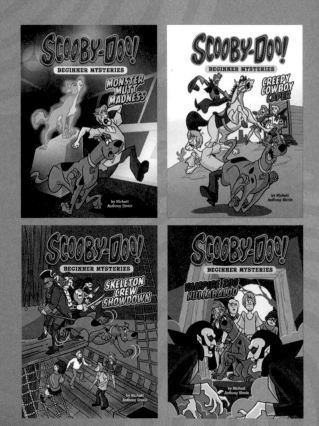